Whispers of Withered Leaves
枯葉の囁き

作・英訳 南 智子　　絵 葉 祥明

Story & Translation : Minami Tomoko　　Illustrations : Yoh Shomei

小雨上がりの裏庭で、色褪せたニシキギの葉が
遠く鈍色の空を見上げています。

In the backyard after a light rain, faded leaves of a spindle tree
peer up towards the dark grey sky.

ケヤキの小枝でヒヨドリたちが、
いつになく甲高い声で鳴き叫んでいます。
そこへメジロやシジュウカラが、あわて顔でやってきます。

*On the twig of a zelkova, bulbul songbirds chirp shriller than usual,
when diminutive white-eyes and titmice come over helter-skelter.*

タブの木陰でリス達が、

石のようにただじっと周囲の様子を見守っています。

ベランダでは老犬スウが、時折耳をそばだてながら

じっと何かを凝視しています。

In the shade of a camphor tree, squirrels reconnoiter, still as stones.

From the porch, venerable dog Suh keeps watch pricking up her ears.

これから何か儀式でも始まるような、

ちょっと気になる光景です。

This odd scene seems a singular ceremony,

a special performance about to begin.

あたりは今、沈黙をすべてと息づく

もう一つの静かな世界が、

まるで合流前の小川のせせらぎのように、

あるいは大海を夢見る河のうねりのように、

何かをひたすら心に秘めながら、

ヒタヒタと音もなく密やかに時を刻んでいます。

All around, another serene world lives in perpetual silence,
steadily and stealthily ticking away cherished time,
like a murmur of a brook before joining the stream,
or meandering rivers yearning to merge with the sea.

たった今、何かがひっそり完結したような、

ちょっと謎めいた情景です。

This enigmatic vision seems something precious about to complete in perfect tranquility.

しばらく張りつめていた静寂を遮るように、
何処からともなく、幽かな声が心に響いたその瞬間、
ニシキギの枯葉がパラパラと風に運ばれていきます。

From thin air a faint intonation touches my soul,
the tense silent soundtrack suddenly broken,
and the shriveled spindle leaves begin to fly away, rustling in the wind.

枝から離れてゆくその姿を無心に見つめていると、

何故か無性に儚くて、そしてちょっぴり空しくて、

まるで自分自身を見送っているような、

不思議な気持ちが侘しさとともに湧いて来て、

ただぼんやりと心の中に"共感"の想いが芽生えてきます。

Contemplating the delicate leaves departing from their branches,

a strange notion swells in my heart, like bidding me goodbye.

From a sad empty loneliness,

I dimly feel empathy germinate within me.

何故か今ぼんやりと、枯葉の心に一瞬寄り添えたような、
ちょっと神秘的な心境です。

それはまるで、"私"から解き放たれた無垢な心が、
大気に溶けていくような
無の中の透明な想いだったのです。

*A mystical sensation overtakes me as if
I could touch the hearts
of these wilted leaves if only for a fleeting moment.*

*It is a transparent feeling of nothingness,
a pure spirit freed from inside,
poised to melt away into the ether.*

もしかすると、あの時聴こえた幽かな声は、
色を極めて旅立って行く"枯葉の囁き"だったのでしょうか。

*Perhaps this faint voice is the whispering of withered leaves
embarking on a new journey,
having surmounted their pinnacle of rich color.*

21

ひょっとすると、あの声は、

別れを惜しみながら先を急ぐ "枯葉の挨拶" だったのかもしれません。

Or perchance a farewell

from those who rush away looking back with regret.

いや多分、あの時響いた幽かな音は、
地球に住むすべてのモノの魂が帰っていく
永遠の一なる場所を暗示する、
宇宙の"沈黙の響き"そのものだったのかもしれません。

May be this utterance is a cosmic communique,
sounding from the one eternal place where
the quintessence of all earthly creations finally returns.

何故か今私の心は、無限なる宇宙の内在意志と
共感・合体してしまったような、実に筆舌しがたい心象なのです。

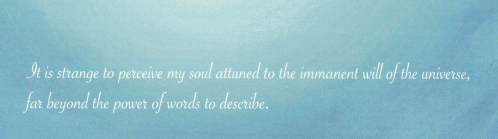

It is strange to perceive my soul attuned to the immanent will of the universe, far beyond the power of words to describe.

そんな夢幻の想いに浸っていると、
ぽっかり抜けた谷戸の空に、長くて曲がりくねった一本の光の道と、
鮮やかな虹色のきざはしが、そして、犬の形をした浮雲が
一瞬私の瞳に映ったような気がしました。

Lost in reverie, an ephemeral tableau appears high in the vast sky above
this mountain hollow, a long and winding luminous road,
a vivid rainbow-hued staircase, and a dog-shaped floating cloud,
beckon . . . . . . then dissolve.

29

あとがき

　一昨年の 11 月、我が家のコーギー犬スウが突然の肺炎で亡くなりました。
　鳥のざわめきにハッとしてベランダに出ますと、東雲の空に柄杓型の北斗七星が涙の如く煌めき、薄らと、指でなぞったような一本の筋雲が道標のように高く天上に伸びていました。
それは、私がこのエッセイを書き上げたほんの数時間後の、まるでおとぎ話のような出来事でした。
　読者の皆様がこの絵本にほんのいっときお心を解き放ち、天空を散歩するようなお気持ちで枯葉の声に耳を傾け、そこに漂うハープの音色やケルトの妖しげな風を、願わくは愛犬スウの先祖たちがかつて駆け巡った故郷ウェールズのうねるような山並みをほんの少しでも作品の蔭に感じ取っていただけましたら幸甚です。

　最後に、私の英訳をブラッシュアップしてくださった写真家ベン・シモンズさんに感謝の意を表するとともに、この作品に心から共感してくださり、素晴らしい絵を施してくださった画家葉祥明さんに、この場をお借りし改めて心よりお礼申し上げます。

南　智子

2019 年 7 月 7 日

Afterword

In November of the year before last, my venerable dog Suh died suddenly of pneumonia.

She was a Pembroke Welsh Corgi.

Startled by the shrill noise of birds, I rushed outside and looked up at the dawn sky.

Then I found right overhead the Big Dipper shining conspicuously like teardrops, and a streak of cloud formed the trace of a fingertip slightly stretching upward, as if creating a guide map to eternity.

It seemed a fairy tale unfolding, all these strange affairs occurring just a few hours after I'd finished writing this essay.

I would be very grateful if you could kindly read this picture book with your mind a bit open and gently touch the hearts of withered leaves imagining the sensation of walking in the air.

I should be very happy if you could somehow conjure the tones of a Celtic harp, with mysterious Gaelic winds blowing amidst the undulating Welsh mountain ranges where Suh's ancestors once played.

In conclusion, along with my gratitude to American photojournalist Ben Simmons who kindly helped my English translation, I would like to express my special thanks to representative illustrator of Japan Yoh Shomei who heartily empathized with this story and kindly accepted my earnest request.

Minami Tomoko
July o7, 2019

南 智子 Minami Tomoko

1954年7月千葉県船橋市生まれ。エッセイスト。国府台女子学院高等部英語科卒、実践女子大学英文学科卒。富士通（株）海外事業本部入社。退職後、夫の海外駐在に帯同、ドイツおよび英国に15年滞在。日英協会会員。「Japan 2001 フェスティバル」ロンドンハイドパークでの開幕に鶴岡八幡宮の流鏑馬披露を企画。2003年「江戸切子華硝展」をロンドンの日本大使館にて開催（ミキモトロンドン支店協力）。2005年日本・EU市民交流年「英国の陶芸家2人展」を黒田陶苑にて開催。2011年「東日本大震災　鎮魂と再生　魂の画家吉田堅治展」を鶴岡八幡宮直会殿で開催（NHKエンタープライズ協力）。鎌倉市在住。

葉 祥明 Yoh Shomei

1946年熊本生まれ。絵本作家・画家・詩人。創作絵本『ぼくのべんちにしろいとり』でデビュー。1990年、創作絵本『風とひょう』でボローニャ国際児童図書展グラフィック賞受賞。1991年、鎌倉市に「北鎌倉葉祥明美術館」、2002年に「葉祥明阿蘇高原絵本美術館」を開館。http://www.yohshomei.com

---

枯葉の囁き
Whispers of Withered Leaves

2019年9月1日　初版発行

作・英訳：南 智子
絵：葉 祥明

発行人：田中愛子
発行所：かまくら春秋社出版事業部
〒248-0006 鎌倉市小町 2-14-7　電話 0467-25-2864
印刷所：ケイアール
装幀・造本：水崎真奈美

ⓒ Minami Tomoko 2019
Printed in japan　ISBN978-4-7740-07